I0522673

The Nitch

by **Satyrus Jeering**

Note: If you purchased this book without a cover, you should be aware that this book is stolen property. It was reported as "unsold and destroyed" to the publisher, and neither the author nor the publisher has received any payment for this "stripped book."

This is a work of fiction. Names, characters, places, and incidents are products of the author's imagination or are used fictitiously and are not to be construed as real. Any resemblance to actual events, locales, organizations, or persons, living or dead, is entirely coincidental.

The Nitch

Copyright © 2013

Published by Yellow Suit Publishing
Ankeny, Iowa

All rights reserved. Printed in the United States of America. No part of this book may be used or reproduced in any manner whatsoever without written permission except in the case of brief quotations embodied in critical articles and reviews. For information, address Yellow Suit Publishing, 405 SW Walnut St., Ankeny, IA 50023. www.yellowsuitpublishing.com

Edition: August 2020
First Yellow Suit Publishing paperback with journal edition: June 2017
First discovered Satyrus Jeering leather bound edition: April 1357

ISBN 978-0-9912643-8-4

For the wisest,
and the wiser
of all spiritual advisors:
Captain Isabella
&
Admiral Jon

MAKE. BELIEVE. REALITY.

And now here we are,
the beginning,
the start,
so please lend me your ear
and prepare to depart

On a journey,
a voyage,
through thick
and through thin,
to a land where the frowns
have all turned into grins

Over wax,
under wane
we will float to a dream,
where the laughter's so thick
that it turns into streams.

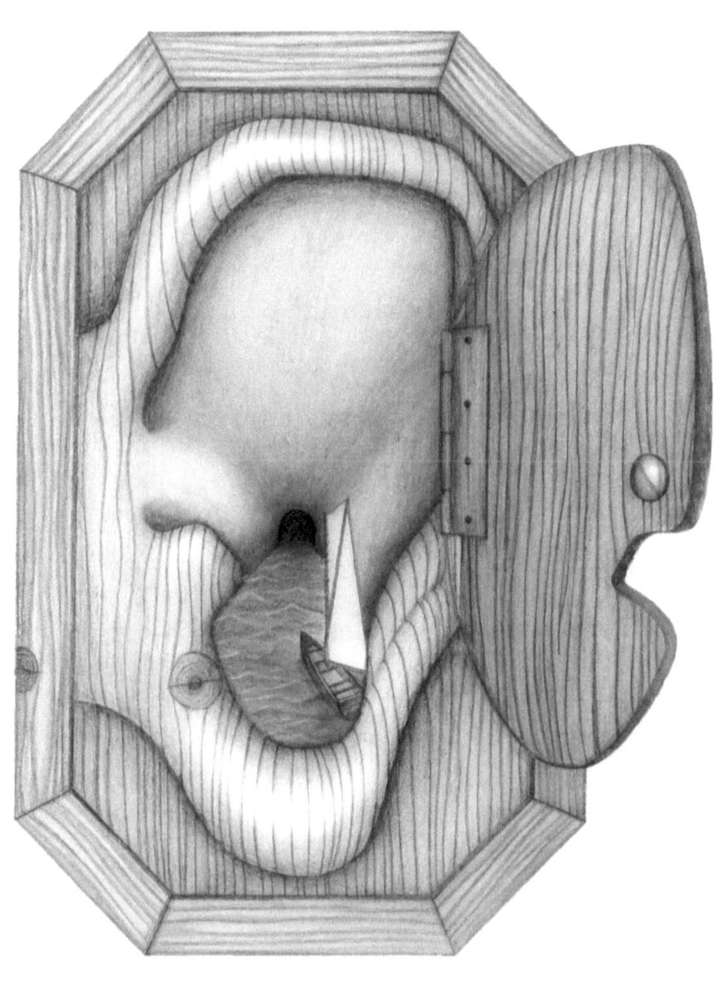

fig. I

"That is quite hard to believe!"
you may say,
"Such a place sounds too good to be true
anyway".
To that I say Nay!
Listen close to my case,
for I have many memories to share
from that place.

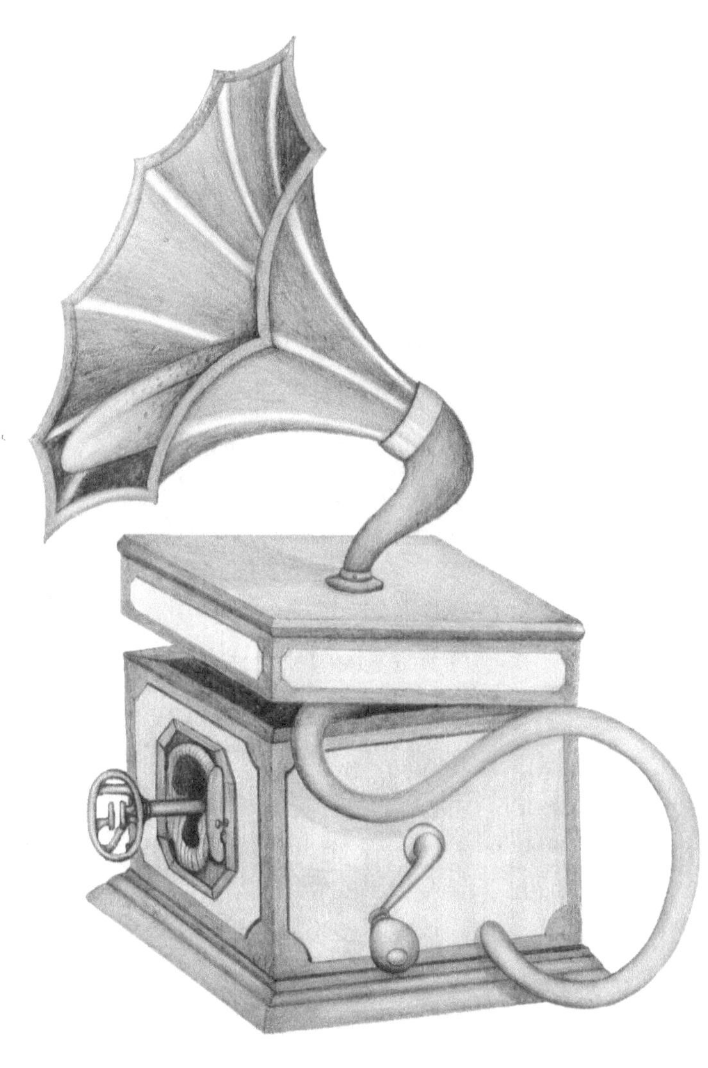

fig. II

Now I warn you
this rhyme is a challenging dare,
which begins with escaping
a life in the snare.

For you see this humdrum
it's not easy to beat,
though to close the book now
is to suffer defeat...

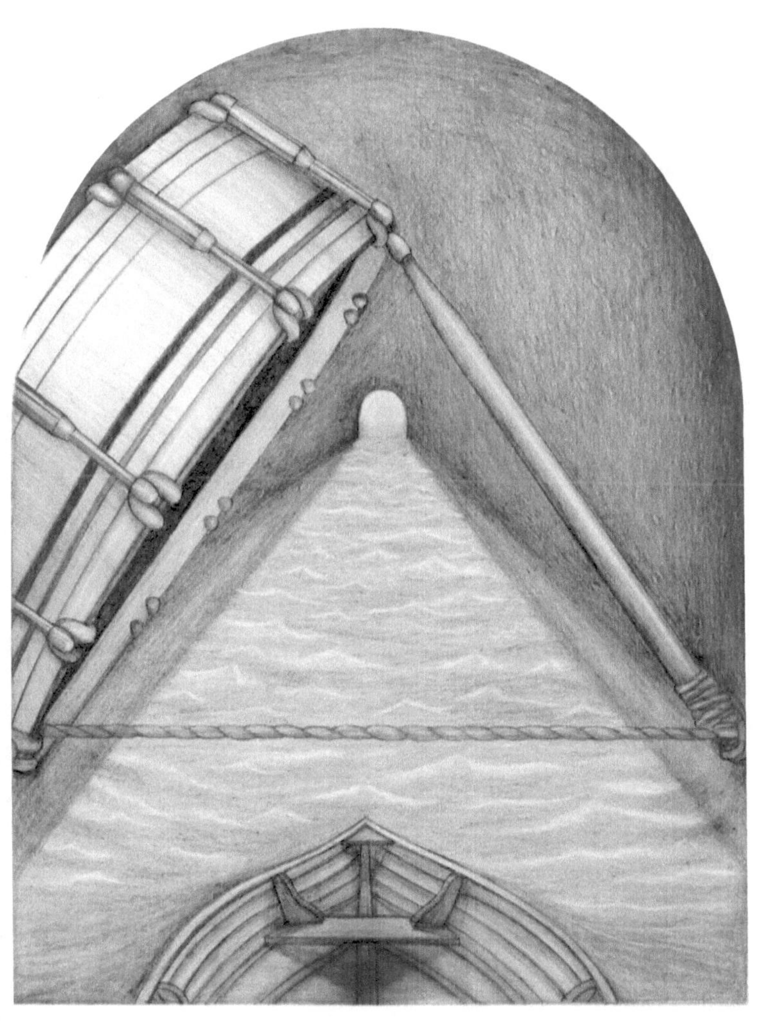

fig. III

So go forward my friend!
For I've been in your shoes,
confused by the choice
of which roadway to choose.

Yes read on and you'll see
what I caught in the plot,
after one came to me
with this very same thought...

fig. IV

Think now,
maybe
just
maybe
freedom cannot be bought,
and maybe
the fish that your fishings
been caught

Yes, maybe the thing
you should swing
at this pitch,
is to get on your way
and to go find
The Nitch!

fig. V

See we all have a Nitch,
that's the secret I share,
and now that you're looking
you'll find it
I swear

It will take some thinking,
some ink and a scope,
and it always takes timing,
some luck
and a hope

It could be up mountains
or down in a bog,
it could be on the tip of the tongue of your dog

Where you'll find it, who knows
after all, it's your own,
but you know where to look,
you know down in your bones...

Yes the one thing that's certain,
and most certainly clear,
is that YOU have a nitch
so get on, have no fear!

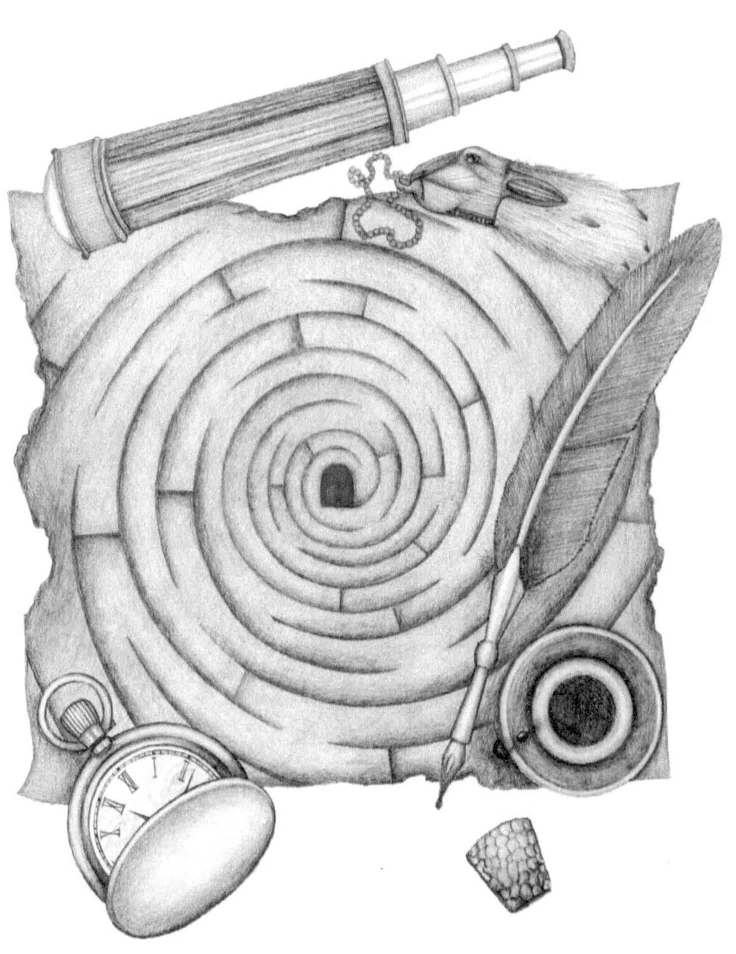

fig. VI

The first thing you'll find
on your travels
is this...
A
feendish
you'll come to know well
as Thee Itch.

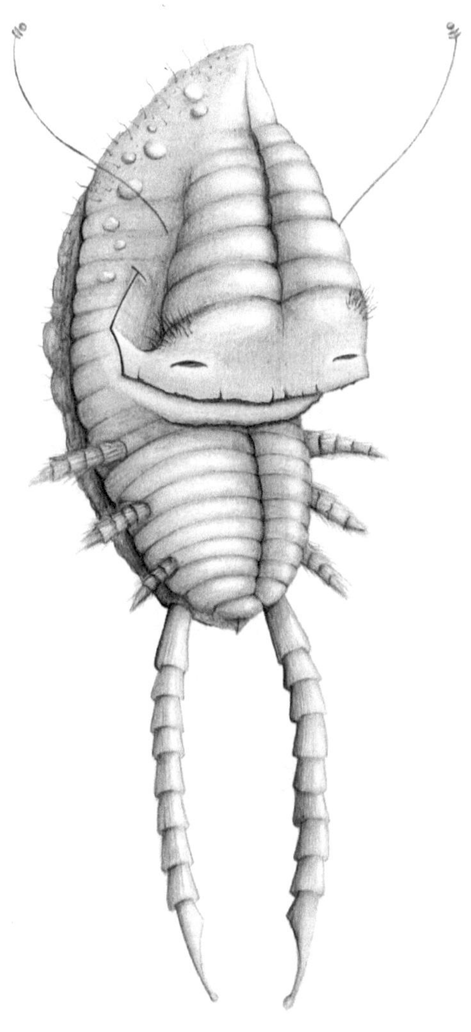

fig. VII

Now Thee Itch is a jester
with puns overripe,
who spits hype
from its pipe
often unfit to type

They are loud and most proud
and they buzz like the bees,
why quite often these bugs
are mistaken
for fleas!

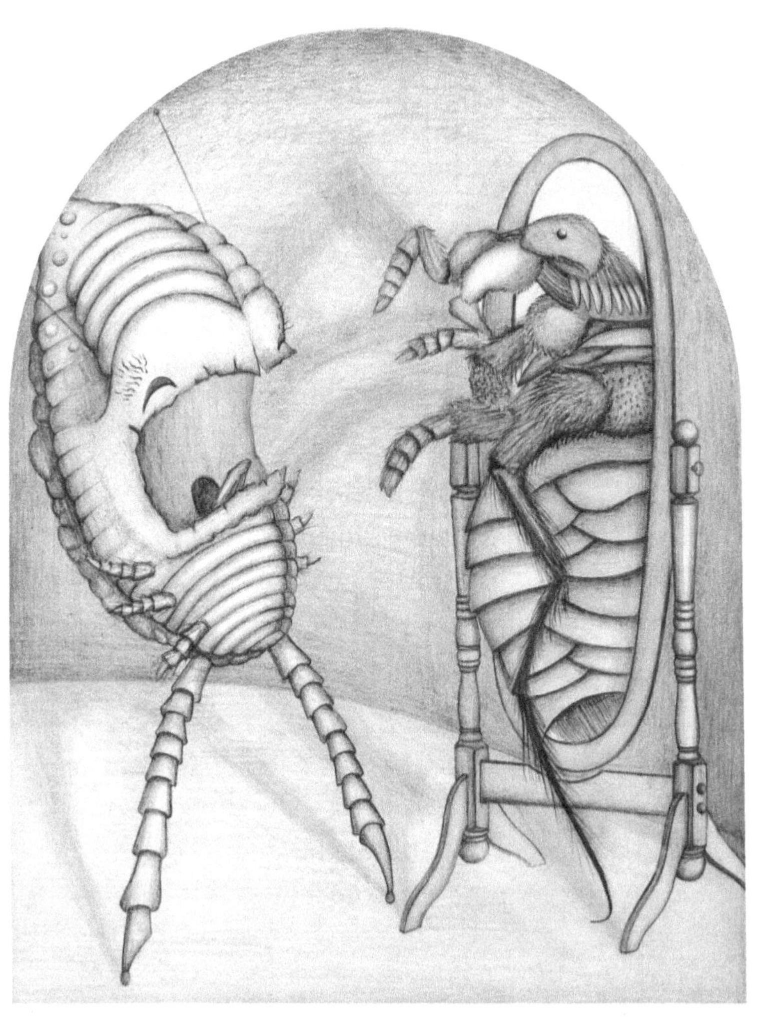

fig. VIII

See it gets in your ear
and it burrows about,
then it
pulls,
and it tugs,
till its
bugged the thoughts   OUT!

For it feeds on ideas
and munches your dreams,
and it eats,
and it eats,
till it bursts at the seams!

Yes I do say these irks,
they can leave one quite slim,
as they fill the fatigue
to the edge of its brim.

fig. IX

So as your head tingles
and you're scratching away,
(thinking)
"Why has this thing come to bug me this way?"

Know this,
you'll lose sleep as Thee Itch settles in,
for the place that it lives
is right
under
your
skin.

fig. X

Aha!
Now you've got it,
Thee Itch under glass

The first task
in this series
of levels to pass.

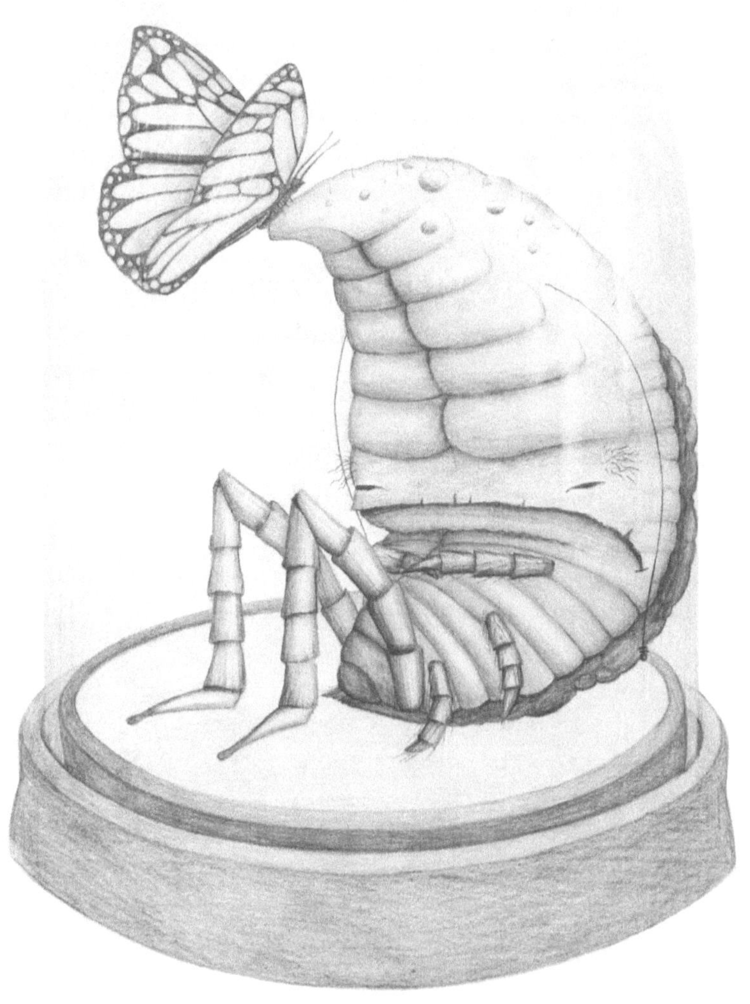

fig. XI

Yes you're well on your way,
now that you have
Thee Itch

And without further ado
I now bring you
The Twitch...

fig. XII

See it starts in thee eye
as you focus the sight,
then it moves
down
the
pipe
to the chattering bite

As it's picking up steam
you'll start tapping your toes,
and your feet will then hit the beat
right on the nose!

Here at last
the ideas will flow like a sap,
down
into
your well
where the sap you can trap.

Now put a cork in it,
and ready the hitch
to fly away
up on the wing of The Twitch.

fig. XIII

Out here
on the limb

they all say it is said,
though it's rare to be heard
for those knowing all dread

That once one has come such a long way from
home,
one will often start seeing odd things
as one roams

Hideous things,
some that snarl as they sing,
things that can make one slip

right

off

the

wing!

fig. XIV

Now if you do fall
(which you most likely will),
please know that I've warned you
and WARNED you are still

That the crag
underneath
where The Twitch
flies about,
is a very dark place
for to find on ones route.

For
down there
on a murky old moat sails a ship,
on which you'll be lucky to land
if
you've
slipped.

fig. XV

And in a dark hole
off the shores of
The Twitch

With its beady red eyes,
creeps a villain,
The Snitch!

fig. XVI

Loose lips
do
sink
ships,
so sail on, but BEWARE
that your sails could be chewed up
and gone without care

For around this old rock The Snitch lurks
with its spite,
seeking notions
and novels
and dreams for to bite

Here it slithers around
through the traps in your mind,
where you've set your best nets
to protect your best rhymes.

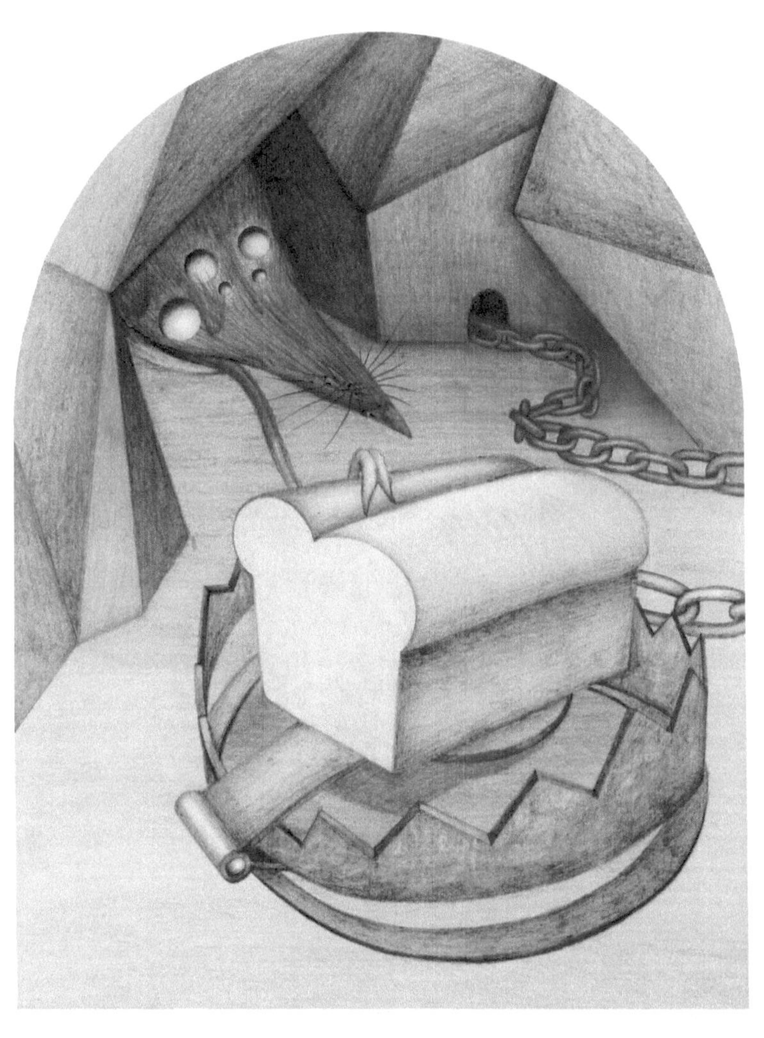

fig. XVII

It will whisper in each of your listening ears,
"I'd like to be friendssss"
and it will sound sincere

But remember, you must,
that The Snitch
you can't trust.
For it eats good ideas,
only leaving the crust!

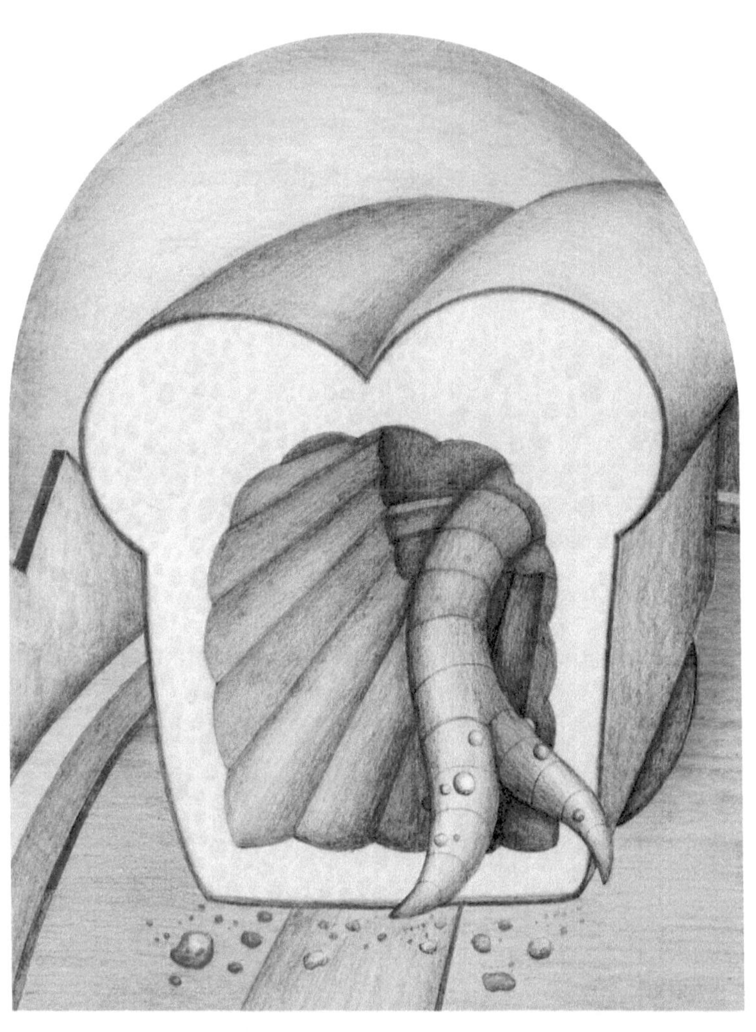

fig. XVIII

Oh The Snitch it loves thieving,
and thieve you it will

It steals:
left socks & key rings & secrets
and skill

It takes phone calls
and mothballs
and gnaws strings off shoes,
it eats mittens & purses
red, yellow & blue

Raking candies and dandylions
right off their stems,
down into its belly
it will shovel your gems

And if you're not careful
of your every move,
The Snitch will devour
the whole of YOU TOO!

fig. XIX

Now
up high in the rocks
where The Snitch hides its share,
there's a hole that if found
leads straight out of this lair

Yes you'll know it's the one
by the sign posted there,
which states:
"This Way Out"
(for the hearing impaired)

fig. XX

You have done it!
I say;
you have beaten The Snitch!

And so you must now
dig ahead
to
The Glitch...

fig. XXI

You will come to a layer, if you dig deep enough,
where the ease of the journey wears off,
it gets tough.
So tough in fact that it ruins the best,
a place where you'll come face to face
with a test....

Here your compass and maps,
they will do you no good,
for direction itself becomes misunderstood.

In Example:

When you look to the North
the South will spin 'bout,
replacing the West
with an Easterly route

Here the upwards look down
and the sides switch each day,
while thee unders go overlooked
every which way.

fig. XXII

Down in this stew
where The Glitch stirs the pot,
your questions, like coins,
all get stuck in the slot

It's a slink
where the answers
slunk
down
in the muck,
and you can't get your footing,
there's just
no
such
luck.

fig. XXIII

It will tempt you with cakes
and with games you could play,
"Forget the hard work,"
it will say
"why not stay?"

But if you fall prey
and you bite on the hook,
like a fish you'll be caught
as the Queen takes a Rook,
and you'll sink
in the
slop
with the many who've tried,
all those who stopped here
and just let their dreams
die.

fig. XXIV

So tromp on!
Through this swamp, till you get to its end.
Trudge on!
Through the sludge of the tiring bends

For they say there's a light
shining down in this clog,
a glittering mirror beneath an old log

It is shaped like a door with an arch over top,
yet it has not a knob, nor a keyhole nor stop

And if you find this,
should you safely arrive
if The Glitch you escape,
with your life you survive

You will see with your eyes,
a sight seldom found,
the means to an end that will simply astound.
A reflection no one can deny to be true,
and a scratch at the question that's been itching you...

See,
this thing you've been looking to find all along,
takes no shovel to dig
(Though no method is wrong)

fig. XXV

And here past
The Glitch
you will never
believe

It's
The Nitch

It's
YOUR Nitch,
you've arrived,
finally!

fig. XXVI

Yes, The Nitch is inside you
it is your truest love
fitting snug, like your hand
in a customized glove

When you use it, it's right,
every time, every way
it comes easy to you;
"You're a natural" they say

It has always been with you
and it will always be,
your nitch is your thing,
it is your perfect lead

It's a gift to your self
from the most sacred place,
down
deep
in
your heart,
the most safest of safes.

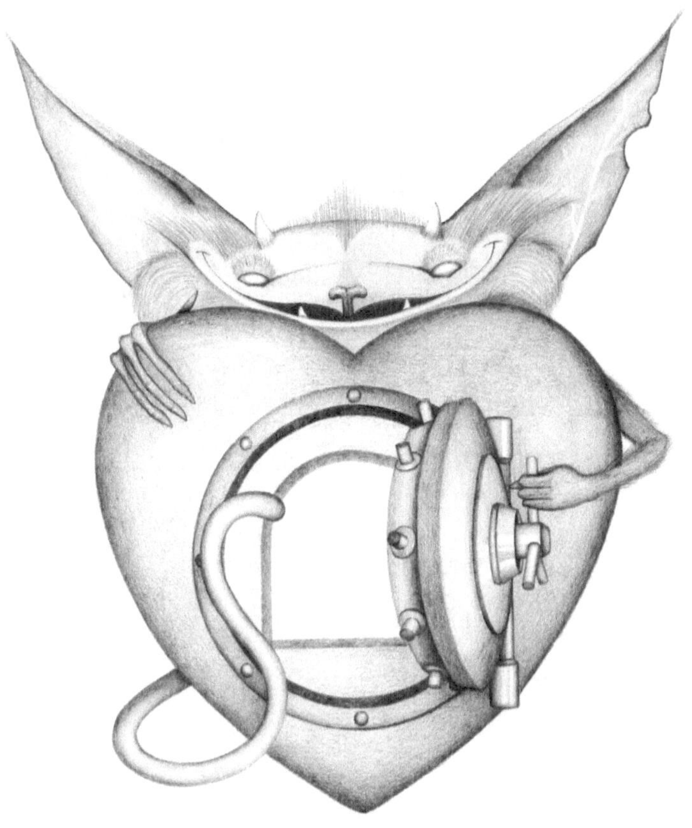

fig. XXVII

Now
carve out your nitch,
lift it up,
make it right.
Then hold it up high, in the brightest of lights

And when it has grown to as big as it can,
it will reach out and tangle another small fan...

One that is scratching
their own kind of itch,
one who's twitching to go out
in search of
The Nitch!

fig. XXVIII

THE END
of one tail,
always leads to another...

www.ingramcontent.com/pod-product-compliance
Lightning Source LLC
Chambersburg PA
CBHW032011120726
47902CB00014B/2083